Horrible Harry
and the Mud Gremlins

Horrible Harry and the Mud Gremlins

BY SUZY KLINE

Pictures by Frank Remkiewicz

SCHOLASTIC INC.

New York   Toronto   London   Auckland   Sydney
Mexico City   New Delhi   Hong Kong   Buenos Aires

ISBN 0-439-56216-3

12 11 10 9 8 7 6 5 4 3 2 1   4 5 6 7 8 9/0

Printed in the U.S.A.   40

First Scholastic printing, April 2004

Set in New Century Schoolbook

Special appreciation to my editor, Cathy Hennessy, and my husband Rufus who helped me write this manuscript.

Also a special thank you to my daughter Emily for her comments, and to Ed Bosman, President of the Connecticut Valley Mycological Society, for an exciting hike in a state park discovering mushrooms!

Other Books by Suzy Kline

Horrible Harry in Room 2B

Horrible Harry and the Green Slime

Horrible Harry and the Ant Invasion

Horrible Harry's Secret

Horrible Harry and the Christmas Surprise

Horrible Harry and the Kickball Wedding

Horrible Harry and the Dungeon

Horrible Harry and the Purple People

Horrible Harry and the Drop of Doom

Horrible Harry Moves Up to Third Grade

Horrible Harry Goes to the Moon

Horrible Harry at Halloween

Horrible Harry Goes to Sea

Horrible Harry and the Dragon War

Song Lee in Room 2B

Song Lee and the Hamster Hunt

Song Lee and the Leech Man

Song Lee and the "I Hate You" Notes

Dedicated with love
To my fourth grandchild,
Saylor Elizabeth Hurtuk, born on July
2, 2002, in Rockville, Connecticut.
I love you, Gamma

Contents

Harry the Fibber　　　　1

Harry's Necklace　　　　5

The Writing Wall　　　　15

To Go or Not to Go?　　　23

Hole in the Fence　　　　32

The Mud Gremlins　　　　41

Horrible Harry
and the Mud Gremlins

Harry the Fibber

I always knew my best friend Harry was a fibber. The good thing was he never fibbed to me, or Song Lee, or our third grade teacher, Miss Mackle. He just fibbed to one person.

Sidney La Fleur.

There's no doubt about it—Sid bugs Harry. One day, Sid sneaked one of Harry's homemade brownies and then had the nerve to ask about the crunchy part. Well, Harry got revenge by telling Sid a fib. He said the crunchy part was a special ingredient he had added.

Cockroaches.

Boy, did Sid flip out! He didn't know it was just chopped almonds.

I thought it was funny. Besides, Sid had it coming. He *can* be annoying! He also has this bad habit of calling Harry a canary. Once Sid put canary stickers on Harry's chair, Harry's lunch box, *and then* Harry's new library book about dinosaurs. Harry got so mad he planned a triple revenge.

Another fib!

It happened after school. Harry told Sid he wanted to shake his hand to thank him for all the canary stickers. When Sid asked why the handshake felt so slimy, Harry told him, "It was a *slug*."

Sid screamed all the way home.

Harry told me later it was just left-over banana from lunch.

Harry's fibs never bothered me before. Usually, they made me laugh. But there was *one fib*—the one I'm going to tell you about—that really bothered me. It gave me goose pimples and made me sweat!

Harry's mud gremlin fib.

The really horrible part was that Harry got all of us—Mary, Ida, Dexter, Sidney, me, and even Song Lee to go along with it.

It all began one Monday morning in November, when Harry wore a necklace to school.

Harry's Necklace

"Hey, Doug," Sidney whispered when he walked into Room 3B, "what's Harry wearing around his neck?"

"It looks like a necklace," I said, hanging up my jacket.

"A necklace?" Sid giggled. After he put his lunch box on the rack, we walked over to the science corner. Harry was standing on our new round yellow moon rug, checking the mold we

were growing. Everyone in Room 3B
had taped a Baggie to the wall with
one slice of bread in it. We had started
the experiment ten days ago.

"Look at the cool green mold!" Harry exclaimed.

Sid was unimpressed. He wanted to talk about Harry's jewelry. "Hey Harry, don't you know that girls wear necklaces? Not boys!"

Just as Harry put a fist up, Mary appeared. "I can't believe you said that, Sidney La Fleur. Don't *you* know boys have been wearing necklaces for *years*? Men too. Didn't you watch the World Series? Half of the baseball players had necklaces on. And what about Michael Jordan? He wears a gold earring."

Sid took a step back, turned, and walked over to the art supply table.

Mary moved closer to Harry and examined his necklace. "Hmm, interesting," she mumbled. "It's hexagonal, six sides. Is that a cover over it?"

"Yup," Harry replied. Now Song Lee, Dexter, and Ida joined us.

"What's underneath the cover?" Ida asked.

"A locket?" Song Lee guessed.

"Nope," Harry answered. "I'll show you."

Very slowly, Harry slid the cover to one side. "My grandma got this for me at the museum shop on Sunday. It's a microscope. See the glass lens? You can look through it."

Mary picked up the end of Harry's silvery chain and looked through the dangling lens. "Wow! I can see the lines on my own finger!"

"Sure you can!" Harry said. "This baby magnifies things ten times."

When Song Lee took a turn, she used

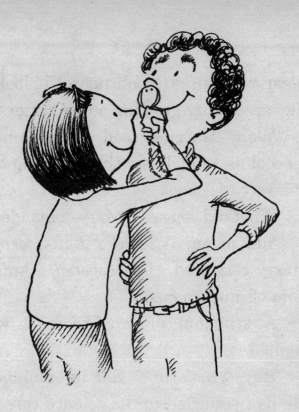

the lens to look at Harry's face. "I can see the black hairs in your nose."

Harry raised one eyebrow. "Want to see *green* hairs? Just look at the bread mold we're growing."

Song Lee looked through the hexagonal magnifying glass into the closest plastic Baggie. "Ooooh neato! It looks like green fuzz growing out of craters."

"Yeah," Harry agreed. "But it's not as cool as what I saw this morning on the way to school."

"What did you see?" Mary demanded.

"You mean, *What did I discover?*" Harry corrected. "I *discovered* a kingdom of mushrooms."

"A kingdom of mushrooms?" we replied.

"Hey, what's up?" Sid interrupted. He had returned to the science corner wearing a yellow yarn necklace. Three paper clips were hanging from it like silver jewels.

No one made a comment. We were too interested in Harry's discovery.

Harry lowered his voice. "Just wait till recess. I'll show you some wicked looking fungi. And you can look at it with my new magnifying necklace."

"What's fun gee?" Sid blurted out.

"Fun *guy*," Harry corrected. "Don't you pay attention in science? Mushrooms are a part of the fungus kingdom, like the bread mold we're growing. My grandma told me we use fungi to make detergent, penicillin for antibiotics, blue cheese, and . . ." Harry flashed his white teeth ". . . salami."

"Aaauugh!" Sid gasped clutching his throat. "Mom made me a salami sandwich today. I'm eating fungi for lunch!"

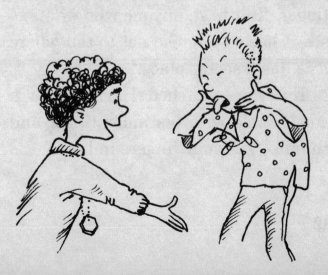

"We're *all* eating it for lunch, Sid," Harry replied. "Yeast is a fungus that's inside bread. But when it's between our toes, it's called athlete's foot. You gotta be tough, Sid!"

Sidney's face turned as green as the mold in our experiment. Harry patted him on the back. "Today's your lucky day, Sid. You get to eat a double fungus sandwich. Salami *and* bread!"

Song Lee giggled. "Can you show us the kingdom of mushrooms at recess?"

"At recess," Harry said holding up a finger. "But first, anyone who wants to see it has to promise not to tell where it is. It's a secret place."

Everyone watched Harry make a small circle with his index finger and thumb. "Put your fingers in here."

One by one we put our index fingers inside. It was a tight fit!

"Now repeat after me," Harry said, lowering his voice and squeezing our fingers. We huddled together on the moon rug and listened.

"I promise . . ." Harry began.

"I promise . . ." we repeated.

"To follow Harry to the kingdom of mushrooms . . ."

"To follow Harry to the kingdom of mushrooms . . ." we answered.

"And never tell anyone where we go."

"And never tell anyone where we go," we repeated.

"Good," Harry said, breaking up our circle of fingers. "At recess, you're going to have the mushroom treat of a lifetime!" Then he tucked his microscope necklace inside his sweater and gave us a toothy smile.

The Writing Wall

It was a bummer being stuck in class all morning. We had to wait three hours until lunch recess. All we really wanted to do was visit the kingdom of mushrooms!

Miss Mackle noticed our long faces. And frowns.

She immediately wrote "Writing Workshop" on the blackboard, then turned around with a big smile. "Sometimes, when we're having a bad day, it's the best day to write!"

Harry and I exchanged a look.

Mary rolled her eyes.

"I want you to write about something that bugs you, and then illustrate it. I'll display your stories and pictures up on a Writing Wall out in the hall."

"Can I make bugs for the wall?" Harry asked.

"Sure! That sounds like fun," Miss Mackle replied. "Just as soon as you finish your story."

Harry's face got longer. He wanted to make bugs first.

"I know what I'm writing about—my brother!" Ida groaned. "He really bugs me."

Miss Mackle smiled. "No names please. But you can write about what a person *does* that bugs you . . . like teasing or yelling or—"

"Smoking," Dexter interrupted. "I hate smoke."

"I'm writing about *lice*," Sidney yelled. "I got them last year. That really *bugged* me."

"What good ideas!" the teacher exclaimed. "Anybody else?"

Song Lee raised her hand. "I remember once my family got dressed up and went to a nice restaurant. There was sticky gum under the table. I hated that!"

Miss Mackle put her hand over her heart.

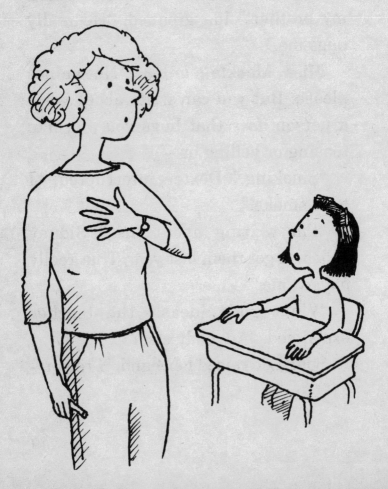

"I've got the worst one," Harry bragged. "Tick bites. My grandma found one on her back last summer after we came back from a hike. That hairy bugger was half in and half out of her skin. As soon as I finish writing about it, I'll make ticks and lice for the writing wall."

While everyone cringed, Ida raised her hand. "I've got another one now. Black ice. My mom and I nearly got in an accident last winter. Our car swerved all over the road!"

Miss Mackle gasped. "Oh no! Let's begin writing now!"

Mary scowled. She couldn't think of anything. I couldn't either.

Then Mary started tapping her pencil.

That's it, I thought. Tapping bugged

me. Finger tapping, pencil tapping, foot tapping . . . I got busy writing.

Thirty minutes later, we shared our stories. One by one we used Miss

Mackle's microphone in the front of the room. Even the teacher read her story aloud. She hated long meetings.

Mary was the only one who didn't share. "I have writers' block," she complained. "All the things I hate have been taken. I don't want to write on the same thing that someone else did. I want to hate something different."

Miss Mackle smiled. "Maybe something will come to you later in the day. I'll call on you then."

Everyone who finished their writing got to look at the green bread mold under the microscopes. Song Lee and I even made slides of the green fuzz.

Finally, at twelve o'clock, the bell rang. We all hurried to the cafeteria and gobbled down our lunches. Sidney traded his salami sandwich for Harry's peanut butter and jelly. Sid said he wanted to eat just a single fungus sandwich. Not a double. When everyone finished, we hustled outside for recess!

To Go or Not to Go?

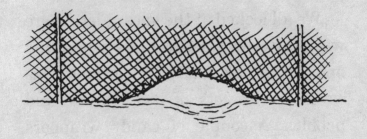

As soon as we got outside on the playground, the six of us gathered around Harry.

"Take us to the kingdom of mushrooms!" Mary demanded.

Harry took his necklace out of his sweater and grinned. "Follow me."

We did. Harry took us to the far end of the playground, the side that faced an empty lot, not the street. "This is it."

Song Lee shrugged. "Where?"

Harry pointed to the other side of the fence.

We all looked at the vacant lot. There was scattered grass, a few bushes, and one white oak tree. The ground was covered with lots of dirt, leaves, and pebbles. A couple of candy wrappers and one crumpled potato chip bag floated in a puddle of water next to a chewed-up tennis ball.

"We can't go over there," Mary snapped. "It's a school rule. You never leave the playground. Can't we see the mushroom kingdom from the fence?"

"Nope," Harry replied. "*The kingdom of mushrooms* is five yards away. Just beyond that oak tree."

"Ooooh," Dexter hummed. Then he started clicking his fingers. "*The king-*

dom of mushrooms. That's got a beat to it!"

Harry lowered his eyebrows. "Haven't any of you ever gotten a ball from the other side of the fence?"

"I did once," I admitted. "In first grade, I crawled under this very fence and got our kickball. The teacher didn't seem mad at all. She just said, 'Don't do it again.' I think she was glad I got our red ball back."

When I pointed to the fence where the wire was pushed back, everyone noticed there was an opening big enough for someone to crawl under.

"I'm not going under there!" Mary said crossing her arms.

"Chicken?" Harry replied.

"I'm not a chicken!" Sidney said, yanking his yarn necklace out from under his jacket. I think he was trying to copy Harry. "I'm tough!"

"Me too," Dexter replied. "When Elvis was in the army, he had to go into dangerous territory. I'm ready."

Harry looked at the girls.

Ida had the same question I did. "What if someone sees us?" she asked. "I don't want to get in trouble."

"No one will see you," Harry insisted. "That's the beauty of my plan."

"What plan?" I asked.

Harry answered right away. "You guys go one at a time. I'll be waiting for you on the other side. Five of you will stand in front of the fence like a human wall. No one will see us back there."

"A human wall . . . cool!" Dexter

replied. Then he added a "bee bop de boo."

I could tell Song Lee was curious about the kingdom of mushrooms. Her fingers were curled around the wire fence, and she gazed longingly at the other side. But I also knew Song Lee had never broken a school rule before.

"Why don't we go after school?" she suggested.

Harry shook his head. "Half of you ride the bus. This is the only time we can all go together."

When Song Lee didn't say anything, Harry knew she was thinking hard. "It's for the sake of science," he pleaded. "It will be our own secret field trip. No one will tell where we went. We made a promise about that. We're not going to Timbuktu. Just a couple of yards beyond the fence!"

Mary put her hands on her hips. "Five yards is not just a couple of yards, Harry Spooger!" she barked. "And what kind of mushrooms are in the kingdom anyway? Ordinary ones like the kind in tuna noodle casserole? I'm not going under the fence to see those boring beige ones!"

Harry pointed a finger at Mary. "I guarantee you the mushrooms are not ordinary. And they're not boring. They're . . . stinkhorns."

"*Stinkhorns?*" we replied.

"They're slimy and smelly, too," Harry added.

Mary took a step back. "I bet I'll hate them."

Harry nodded. "Probably. But if you hate them, you'll have something to write about."

Mary made a tent with the tips of her fingers. "Hmmm," she mumbled,

tapping them slowly together. "Miss Mackle is expecting a story from me this afternoon. And it would be something different. I don't want to let her down. Maybe I will make a quick visit to see the stinkhorns."

Then she added, "But *if* I do, I'm going last!"

Hole in the Fence

Sidney scooted under the fence while the rest of us made our human wall.

"Act like nothing's happening," Mary snapped.

Suddenly, we heard groans coming from Sidney. After he crawled back under the fence, he swayed back and forth. "Aauuugh, that smell. . . . Stinkhorns are so gross!" The next thing he did was fall flat on the playground like he was dead.

"Get up, Sid!" Mary scolded. "You'll call attention to what we're doing!"

Sidney acted like Mary was a drill sergeant. He jumped up, clicked his heels together, and joined our human

wall. Dexter scooted through the hole, and then Ida went.

When I looked at my watch, I noticed we didn't have much recess left. "Song Lee," I said, "you and I had better go

together. There won't be enough time otherwise."

Song Lee agreed. She and I scrambled under the fence then raced over to Harry. He was kneeling on the ground

behind the tree. "Welcome to the kingdom of mushrooms, guys! Take a look at these babies."

Song Lee's eyes were as big as mine!

It was like nothing we had ever seen before. Ten mushrooms poked through the earth like white thumbs wearing olive green slimy helmets.

"Stinkhorn mushrooms are cool, huh?" Harry exclaimed.

Song Lee giggled and nodded. She loved slimy things, like Harry did. I wasn't so crazy about them.

"My grandma and I spotted a whole bunch of them on our hike last Sunday in the woods," Harry explained. "She has this neat mushroom guidebook and is teaching me the names. Smell the top of them."

Song Lee kneeled down and put her

nose real close. After she inhaled, she smiled at Harry. "I'll take this one back with me to make a slide."

"Aaauughuuuuuuuugh!" I groaned. "These mushrooms smell worse than rotten eggs. No wonder the flies are buzzing around here."

"It's a putrid smell," Harry explained. "That's what Grandma says."

The putrid smell didn't seem to bother Song Lee. She used Harry's magnifying glass to get an even closer look. "There are tiny holes in the stem, like sponge!"

"Yeah," Harry agreed.

"Hurry up, you two!" Mary whispered. "The bell's going to ring any minute now, and I won't get a turn."

Song Lee ripped off a small part of the olive green cap as we hurried back under the fence.

"Three years later," Mary snarled, "it's finally *my* turn!"

We all watched Mary get down on her knees and try to squeeze under the wire fence. She had a little trouble, so we gave her rear end a nudge with the backs of our legs.

She wasn't gone long.

When she returned, she had one comment. "I know why they call them stinkhorns. They stink!"

Just as the bell rang, Harry popped up. We slapped each other five, then raced across the playground. "I told you it would be a piece of cake," Harry bragged.

When we got back to the classroom, we had fifteen minutes of activity time. No one said anything that made us nervous. Song Lee and I made another slide with the specimen from the stinkhorn.

Harry got out the *I* encyclopedia for *insects*. He wanted to draw lice and ticks for the writing wall.

Suddenly the teacher's voice shattered our concentration. "Who's tracking in all this mud on our brand-new yellow

moon rug?" the teacher asked. "Just look at those dirty footprints! Where could they have come from? There's no mud on the playground. It's asphalt."

We all looked desperately at Harry.

"The mud gremlins?" he mumbled.

The Mud Gremlins

Miss Mackle didn't laugh when Harry said mud gremlins. We didn't either. We all knew it was a big fat fib, but not one of us said a word.

"Who are the mud gremlins?" Miss Mackle asked.

Harry hemmed and hawed a bit. Then he explained. "When we don't know who did something at my house, we usually blame it on the gremlins.

My great grandfather Sam Spooger always told me that during World War II when things went wrong with his plane, everyone blamed it on the gremlins. They're little creatures that mess things up."

Miss Mackle managed a small smile. "The gremlins, huh?"

"Yeah," Harry continued. "They even take things at my house, like socks and keys. I bet they tracked in mud on our classroom rug."

"I don't think so," the teacher replied. "Maybe they take your socks, Harry, but they didn't track in this mud. Does anyone else have an explanation for this mess?"

The class looked at the brown footprints that crossed over the yellow moon rug several times.

Mary immediately went to her seat and started writing.

Song Lee turned off the microscope and hurried over to her desk. When she put her head down, I knew what she was thinking.

The same thing I was thinking.

Telling a gremlin fib was one thing. Keeping the truth from our teacher was another. We all knew what *the truth* was, too! We were the ones who tracked in mud. We broke a school rule by going under the fence and into the empty lot without permission.

The teacher waited patiently for someone to say something. It was a very long, uncomfortable silence.

I could feel the goose bumps popping up on my arms. I could also feel the wet sweat dripping down the sides of my face.

"I feel sick," Song Lee blurted out. "Please, may I go to nurse's office?"

I knew it. Song Lee felt awful, too.

Just as Song Lee got to the doorway, Mary jumped out of her seat. "Wait! We'll all feel better if I read this now."

Song Lee turned around and listened with the rest of us.

Mary cleared her throat, then read her paper.

I hate stinkhorn mushrooms. They're smelly and ugly. But more than that I hate fibbing. It can make you sick. You let people down, like your nice teacher. I'm one of the mud gremlins that sneaked through the hole in the fence at recess to see a stinkhorn mushroom. Because it rained last night, the dirt in the lot stuck to my shoes. I made a real mess out of everything, and not just our classroom rug. I am very sorry. I hate fibbing!

As soon as Mary read her story,
Song Lee ran into the teacher's arms.
"I am a mud gremlin, too. I'm so sorry,
Miss Mackle."

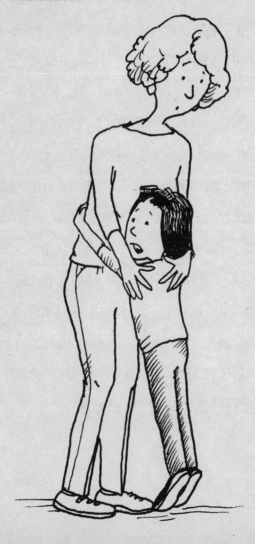

Dexter and I showed the teacher the bottoms of our shoes. "We did it, too," we said. "We're sorry."

"Me too," Ida said.

Sidney whispered something, but no one could hear him.

Harry bowed his head. "It's all my fault, Miss Mackle. I got everyone to go under the fence to see the fungi. I'm real sorry."

The teacher folded her arms as she looked at Harry. "Well," she groaned, "I accept the apologies of the mud gremlins. Each one of you seems to have genuine remorse. I'm glad Mary and now the rest of you are telling me the truth. That's what's most important. But this is no laughing matter. You broke an important school rule. You went on that little science field trip *without* permission. There will be consequences. I'll be calling your parents. And you'll have to stay after school today."

All of us nodded, while Harry reached for the hand broom. "I'll start cleaning the dirt off the rug, Miss Mackle."

"I will help Harry," Song Lee said reaching for the dustpan. She seemed to be feeling a little better.

"I'll help, too," I said.

That day after school, we did chores for one hour. Harry and I used scrub brushes to clean the new moon rug real well with soap and water. Then we washed the blackboards and all the desktops with big purple sponges.

Song Lee, Ida, and Mary rearranged all the books in our two large bookcases. One was for fiction and the other was for nonfiction. Dexter and Sidney swept the floor and cleaned out the teacher's closet.

The worst part was facing our parents afterward.

The best part was that the girls found more neat books about mushrooms and fungi in our own classroom library. And Sidney found a lunch bag that was in the teacher's closet. Inside was an old orange. It had grown an

amazing layer of green and white mold. Miss Mackle let us look at it with Harry's magnifying necklace. Song Lee even made a slide of it.

But the very best part was that Miss Mackle planned a visit to a nearby state park where there were all kinds of mushrooms, and *everyone* remembered to bring a permission slip. Even Harry.